The Winter King

Look for these other Dean Morrissey books:

A Christmas Carol

The Christmas Ship

The Moon Robber

The Magic Door Series
BOOK 2

The Winter King

By Dean Morrissey and Stephen Krensky
Pictures by Dean Morrissey

 HarperCollins*Publishers*

For Toni Markiet

Library of Congress Cataloging-in-Publication Data
Morrissey, Dean
The winter king / by Dean Morrissey and Stephen Krensky ; pictures by Dean Morrissey.
p.   cm. — (The magic door series ; bk.2)
Summary: When Sarah sneaks aboard Old Man Winter's wagon and travels with him
through the magic door to the Great Kettles, she must help him stop his power-hungry
assistant from taking over the weather making for his own purposes.
ISBN 0-06-028583-4 — ISBN 0-06-028584-2 (lib. bdg.)
[1. Weather—Fiction. 2. Winter—Fiction. 3. Space and time—Fiction.
4. Magic—Fiction.] I. Krensky, Stephen. II. Title.
00-046099
[Fic]—dc21   CIP
AC

Typography by Stephanie Bart-Horvath
1 2 3 4 5 6 7 8 9 10

First Edition

CHAPTER ONE

"Give me a hand with his head," said Sarah.

She was speaking to her friend Michael. Together they knelt down and lifted a ball of snow, balancing it carefully on top of two others.

"There!" said Michael. "All we need now is a scarf, a hat, and a carrot."

"It's too bad snowmen can't talk," said Sarah.

"Why?" asked Michael.

"Because then we could ask him what's up with the weather. We don't often get this much snow all at once. And did you hear about that blizzard in Florida? Or the ice storm out west in the desert?"

Instead of answering, Michael grabbed Sarah's arm, pointing toward the street. A huge horse had rounded the corner pulling an old wooden wagon. Snow clung to the dark fabric of the driver's coat and seemed to mingle with his white hair and beard.

While Michael and Sarah stood staring, the wagon passed slowly by, the horse's hooves clomping softly on the snowy street. Then it turned the next corner and disappeared.

"MICHAEL!" shouted a voice from down the street.

"Uh-oh," said Michael. "That's my dad. I was supposed to shovel the driveway right after school. I'd better go."

Sarah frowned. "I thought we were going to work on our weather project at the library."

"You go ahead. I'll catch up."

"Well, you'd better hurry. This time we're going to beat Cordelia."

Cordelia Tuck was in their fifth-grade class. Her father ran a research lab, and every time the class did science projects, Cordelia's was always the best. Sarah was convinced Cordelia somehow got help from a team of her father's best scientists, working deep into the night in their underground fortress.

Waving good-bye to Michael, Sarah headed for the library. On the way she passed The Magic Door

Toyshop. Sarah usually stopped in to say hello to her friend Sam Thacher, the owner and the best toy maker in town.

But today she stopped for another reason. The wagon she and Michael had seen earlier was now standing in front of the shop. The horse was stamping its feet restlessly and breathing out puffs of white fog into the air.

"Sam?" Sarah cried, bursting through the front door. "Have you see the wagon and the horse outside?"

"Yes, I have," said the toy maker, rising from his bench. "And don't take the roof off shouting. We need it on a day like this."

"Is there a problem with my wagon?" said a visitor, stepping forward into the light.

Sarah jumped. She recognized the driver at once. He smiled politely at Sarah, but it was not a warm smile. Nothing about the man seemed warm.

"Sarah," said Sam, "this is a friend of mine, Ira McHoul."

"Nice to meet you," said Sarah, remembering her manners. "If you leave your wagon out there, you'll get a parking ticket for sure."

"A ticket?"

Sarah looked doubtfully at Mr. McHoul. "You must be from out of town."

He nodded. "You could say that."

"Wait a minute!" Sarah exclaimed. "You're from the Kettles!"

Mr. McHoul cocked an eyebrow at Sam.

"Sarah's been there," Sam explained. "That business with the moon I told you about."

"That business with the moon" had been the most exciting adventure of Sarah's life. Together with Michael and their young friend, Joey, she had visited the Great Kettles, a group of islands across the Sea of Time. Everything in the Kettles was wonderful or strange or scary or maybe all three mixed together. But it was never ordinary, like home. Sarah longed to go back, but whenever she asked about it, Sam would say only that the time was not yet right.

Sam himself was from the Kettles. Long ago he had been apprenticed to the Sandman. His job had been to repair the toys that the Sandman found left behind in children's dreams. Eventually, Sam had opened a toy shop in the Great Kettles. But he'd also wanted to share his toys with children in The Outland, which is what people from the Kettles called

Sarah's world. So Sam had left the Kettles through a magic door in his shop and come to Old Bridgeport. That door, nestled comfortably in the wall, remained a gateway back to the Kettles.

"Well, then, maybe young Sarah should listen too." Mr. McHoul sat down with a sigh. "As I was telling Sam, I've reached a patch of rough sledding. A rascal called Kudgel is trying to take over my job. Long ago, Sarah, he was my assistant. But he was always better at stirring up trouble than anything else. I gave him chance after chance, but after a time I had to ask him to leave.

"A few months ago he returned, claiming to have changed his ways. I suppose I should have known better, but I took him back. And this time he did study hard. The more he learned, though, the more he pestered me for a chance to make some winter weather himself."

"You can make weather?" asked Sarah.

"Indeed," said Mr. McHoul. "It is my job, after all. That's why most people call me Old Man Winter. The snow and ice both here and in the Great Kettles come from the Weather Mill at my home in Weathermore Castle. The Weather Mill can create

any kind of storm you might fancy—sleet or snow, or freezing rain."

"So what exactly did Kudgel do?" asked Sam.

"Well, I finally let him try out a small flurry. The result was disastrous. He made such a mess of the calculations that the flurry became a blizzard. I had to leave the castle to repair the damage."

"Couldn't you just fix the Weather Mill?" asked Sarah.

"Unfortunately not. The Mill can make weather, but it cannot change any that has been released. So with my wagon and horse, I rode the rim of the storms, steering them out to sea or into the mountains. I have traveled far fixing Kudgel's mistakes." Old Man Winter sighed. "But he's up to something more. I can feel it like icicles pricking my skin. Ever since I left the castle, he's used the Weather Mill to start one storm after another. I've been on the move ever since, trying to put things right. I haven't had time to return to the Great Kettles and deal with Kudgel—until now."

"So Kudgel has the Weather Mill and all the ingredients he needs," said Sam. "Does he have your recipes as well?"

McHoul shook his head. "The *Book of Storms* remains hidden. But now I must return home and stop Kudgel before he brews up more mischief. Still, I am glad for the chance to stop here briefly and gather my strength."

"Kudgel may not go gently," Sam warned.

Old Man Winter sighed. "I know. But I will deal with that when the time comes."

CHAPTER TWO

"Just a little more."

In the Storm Chamber of Weathermore Castle, a tall figure tapped chalky grains from a glass tube into a wide bowl. He then placed the bowl above a wood fire, watching as the liquid inside began to bubble.

His assistant hovered to one side. "Careful, Master... careful."

"Stop hovering, Numlock," the taller man snapped. "You're worse than a mother hen. I know what I'm doing."

"Of course, Master Kudgel. I never doubted it. You are a genius, a—"

"Numlock!"

"Silence is called for. Concentration. I understand. I will be as quiet as a mouse, a mouse in slippers."

As the grains dissolved, the bubbly liquid turned a silver color.

"Excellent!" said Kudgel. "Now for the final touch."

He added a few drops of a soupy green liquid. *POOUUUFFF!*

The bowl cracked in a puff of smoke. Kudgel staggered back, coughing and waving his arms.

The smoke took a few moments to clear. It left behind a particularly nasty smell.

"Confound McHoul and his tricky recipes," Kudgel snarled. "How can I make suitable weather without the *Book of Storms?*"

"Patience, Master," advised Numlock. "There was much less smoke than last time."

"Kudgel!" The deep, angry voice came from outside.

"He's come back," said Numlock, clapping his hands. "At last."

"I have ears, Numlock," Kudgel said drily. "Tell me, is everything ready? Good. Come, then—we don't want to keep our visitor waiting."

When Kudgel appeared on the castle parapet, Old Man Winter stood up in his wagon across the moat. "Lower the drawbridge at once!" he shouted. "You have acted most unwisely. Your foolishness might have led to tragedy and disaster."

Kudgel looked down thoughtfully. "*Might have led?* You stopped this from happening? A pity."

Old Man Winter frowned. "Have you grown that uncaring? I had no idea. But if you leave the castle now, I will let you go freely."

Kudgel laughed. "How generous. How merciful. But you truly do not understand how things have changed. I am the master now. You were content to waste the power of the Weather Mill, making ice and snowstorms that quickly melted away. I am not so weak. I will be the ruler of winter, and everyone from the Great Kettles to The Outland will fear and obey me. I will be the *Winter King*."

Old Man Winter's face turned white with rage. "You are mad!" he roared. His voice bounced off the raised drawbridge, cracking great chunks of ice loose and rattling the lever and chains. A moment later the drawbridge came loose and crashed down across the moat.

Flicking the reins, Old Man Winter drove the horse onto the wooden bridge.

As Old Man Winter drove under the gate, Kudgel raised his arm. At this signal, Numlock, hidden out of sight above the gate, dumped several barrels of water down over the bridge. They drenched Old Man Winter when he passed beneath.

The horse came to an abrupt stop just inside the castle courtyard. Sitting on the wagon seat behind them was Old Man Winter—encased in a solid block of ice.

"Quickly, Numlock, quickly!" Kudgel shouted. "The ice won't hold the old fool for long. We have only a few minutes."

Numlock dropped a huge net over the giant slab of ice. Then he and Kudgel dragged the ice, with Old Man Winter inside, over to an iron grate in the floor of the courtyard. Numlock pulled the grate aside, and then Kudgel pushed the block of ice down the hole, where it disappeared from sight.

CHAPTER THREE

Old Man Winter's wagon and horse remained alone in the castle courtyard. At least they appeared to be alone. But then one of the blankets in the back of the wagon began to move.

A moment later Sarah poked her head out and cautiously sat up.

When Sarah had left Sam and Old Man Winter, she had been planning to continue on to the library. But as she had passed the wagon and noticed the blankets piled in the back, she had stopped. Who knew when she would get another chance like this? Sarah didn't know if "the time was right," as Sam had put it, but she couldn't pass up the chance to see the Great Kettles again.

At first Sarah had been jolted and rocked, but then the ride had become smoother. There were no bumps, no bouncing, only a gentle swaying, as though she were riding on air.

And then the bumpiness had returned, until the wagon creaked to a halt. Sarah had peeked out just before Kudgel and Old Man Winter had exchanged words, catching a glimpse of the forbidding castle and the snowy mountains beyond.

After that she hadn't dared to move until now. There was no sound from outside. Everything seemed very still. Quietly, Sarah climbed out of the wagon. She didn't know what had happened to Old Man

Winter, but she was pretty sure it wasn't good. The question was, what could she do about it?

"Who are you?"

Sarah jumped. Turning, she saw a boy of her own age looking at her from around a corner of the wagon. His sharp eyes were studying her closely.

"I'm Sarah," she said.

"My name's Jack. I see you're not from hereabouts."

"No, I'm from . . . far away."

"I see," said Jack. "In those clothes you could be from Mirth, the village of clowns and jesters. But if I had to guess, I'd say you were from The Outland."

"You know about The Outland?"

Jack nodded. "Never been there myself, but someday I will. How did you get here?"

"I stowed away in the back of this wagon," Sarah explained. "Old Man Winter didn't know I was there. Then Kudgel did something—I don't know what— but he was very happy about it."

"Hmmph!" said Jack. "I thought as much. His cackles echoed all through the castle."

He stepped out from behind the wagon, his foot stepping through a puddle of water. Instantly, white frost crackled across its surface.

Sarah gasped. "Look!" she said.

Jack shrugged. "Oh, that? Happens all the time."

"Really?" said Sarah. She paused. "You said your name was Jack. What's your last name?"

"Frost."

"Jack Frost? *The* Jack Frost?"

"Well, the only one I know," said Jack. "I'm a student of Old Man Winter's. I'm his best student—well, actually, I'm his only student. But no more questions now. If you really want to help, we need to get you some different clothes. Right now you stick out like a third eye. Hmmmm . . . we're about the same size."

"But what about Old Man Winter?"

"Yes, yes," said Jack, glancing around. "Later. First we have to get you changed."

He led Sarah to a servant's wardrobe, where she tried on several things before settling on a tunic, a cap, and a pair of trousers. Then Jack took her up on a deserted parapet. Everywhere Sarah looked, she could see signs of Kudgel's experiments. Trees lay uprooted; shattered boulders sat in piles. The ground was pitted and scarred with great icy fissures.

Then Sarah looked down at the moat—and laughed.

"What's so funny?" asked Jack.

"It's the moat. It's frozen."

Now it was Jack who laughed. "Well, of course it's frozen. What else would you expect here?"

"Yes . . . well, that's true," Sarah admitted. "But I mean, what good is a frozen moat? Anyone could lower himself down with a ladder, walk across, and go up again."

"Is that so?" Jack folded his arms. "Take another look."

As Sarah leaned over the wall for a closer look, a polar bear came sliding around the tower wall. It looked so funny that Sarah almost laughed again. Almost, because the bear suddenly looked up and growled, showing rows of sharp teeth.

"Oh!" Sarah gasped. "Can it get out?"

"No, the moat's sides are too steep and slippery. But you can understand why no one tries to cross it your way."

Sarah nodded. "Old Man Winter is very clever."

"Not clever enough to keep from being captured somehow."

"I wish I had seen something," said Sarah. "It was hard to hear under the blankets, and if I had stuck my head out, they might have seen me."

"You don't have to convince me," said Jack. "Kudgel's caused plenty of trouble already. Up to now it's been safer to stay out of his way. But I can't do that anymore."

"No," said Sarah. "We have to find Old Man Winter—and fast. I have a feeling that the longer he's missing, the worse things will get."

CHAPTER FOUR

"Planning," Kudgel said as he stood in the middle of the Storm Chamber. "Planning and execution."

Numlock smiled broadly. "That was very clever, Master, using Old Man Winter's own power against him."

Kudgel cackled. "Yes, it was, wasn't it? I knew he would get colder than a midwinter blizzard if he got really mad. And so when you poured water over him, he naturally froze up like a giant icicle."

"And now," said Numlock, "we have him where he can't possibly escape, even after he calms down."

Kudgel nodded. "Still, he's a crafty old man. We'll check on him later. For now let's get back to work. It's time to send a message to people here and in The Outland. From now on they'll serve me as the Winter King—or winter will be the only season they ever know."

Kudgel gave a final stir to a sticky mixture in a large bowl. "It's supposed to look like oatmeal," he muttered. He flicked a spoonful at the wall. The glop stuck briefly before dripping down to the floor.

"Perfect," said Kudgel. "Open the Ice Dome. I'm going to unleash a truly terrible storm."

"Yes, Master." Numlock released the stone counterweight. Wooden gears began to turn slowly, and the immense dome lifted up like a great drawbridge.

The Weather Mill was now open on three sides to the sky.

Kudgel craned his neck upward. "Increase the trajectory, Numlock. We have to aim higher."

"But Master, that will mean shooting the mixture almost straight up."

"I know that," Kudgel snapped. "But the high winds above the castle should carry it safely away."

Numlock turned the great crank on the Weather Mill several notches.

"Now, fire!"

Numlock spun the gears to the highest setting and then pulled a lever. A silver ball rolled down a wooden chute and dropped into a hole. The Weather Mill's gears started turning rapidly. Carefully, Kudgel poured the gooey gray mixture into a funnel. It passed through several glass pipes and tubes before disappearing inside. The Mill began to rumble and hum, and the winding shaft spun wildly.

Suddenly—*BOOM!*—a white mass shot out the top of the Weather Mill and up into the sky.

"How long?" Numlock wondered.

"Soon enough," said Kudgel. "It will be like fireworks—only with snow."

Numlock cocked an ear upward. "Do you hear that?"

"What?"

"That noise." Numlock frowned for a moment. "It's kind of a whooshing sound. Like something falling at great speed. Like . . ."

A great comet of snow was rushing down at them. Its shadow was blotting out the sky. There was no place to run or hide.

The giant snowball smashed into the floor with a smacking sound, splattering everywhere.

For a moment there was complete silence.

"Oh, my!" said Numlock, slowly standing up. He looked a little like a melting snowman as he wiped some sleet from his cheek.

Kudgel shook himself like a wet dog and stumbled to his feet. Slush dripped from his face and clothes. "That was not a very good idea, Numlock," he snarled.

"Master?"

"Increasing the trajectory like that."

"But, Master, it wasn't my . . . I mean . . ."

Kudgel eyed his assistant darkly. "Are you suggesting someone else was to blame?"

"Um, no, Master. I don't know what I was thinking of."

"Then stop arguing and GET THIS MESS CLEANED UP!" And with that he swept out of the room.

"Yes, Master! At once!"

Numlock trotted out into the hall to call for a servant. He saw a small figure in tunic and trousers just descending the stairs.

"You, there! Girl!"

"Who, me?" said Sarah. She and Jack had been searching the castle for Old Man Winter. Jack was still in the East Tower, but she had come down to look near the Storm Chamber.

"Of course, you! I'm not talking to myself. Come here."

"Yes, sir," said Sarah. Seeing no way out, she meekly followed Numlock back into the laboratory.

CHAPTER FIVE

Snow and slush were melting in piles around tables and chairs, making icy puddles on the floor.

"Don't touch anything," said Numlock. "And be careful where you step near the Weather Mill."

Sarah gazed up at the great contraption, which filled the middle of the Storm Chamber. Across the front, dials and levers and brass tubes ran every which way.

"Oh, my!" she gasped.

"Now, now, don't be nervous," said Numlock. "The Mill doesn't bite." He stared at her. "I don't seem to recognize you, girl."

Sarah lowered her head. "No, sir, you wouldn't. I've, um, just recently arrived."

"Ah, well, that explains it, then." Numlock shrugged. "Can't know everyone straight away, not a man in my position."

"No, sir," said Sarah. She took another look at the Weather Mill. "Do you know how to run this great thing?"

Numlock smiled. "Indeed I do. Of course, it's not something everyone could manage."

"It looks awfully complicated," Sarah said admiringly. Maybe if she flattered Numlock, she could get him talking and learn something useful.

Numlock puffed out his chest. "Well, yes, that's true." He walked over to a tall cabinet with hundreds of little drawers. "Over here is where we keep the ingredients. On the main panel itself are the controls for snow or sleet or freezing rain. We can also set a storm's intensity and how long it will last. And this device—"

"NUMLOCK!" came a shout echoing down the halls.

"Ah," said Numlock quickly, "there's the Master now. Always wanting my advice on one thing or another. Now, as you can see," he added pointing to the globs of snow, "there's cleaning to be done."

"NUMLOCK, COME HERE THIS VERY INSTANT."

"You see?" said Numlock. "Can't manage without

me, not even for a minute." He pointed to a mop and bucket in the corner. "You start working."

"Me?"

"Of course. I'll be back later to inspect."

Sarah sighed. It was hard to believe she had come all the way to the Great Kettles to clean up melting snow. But for the moment she had no choice.

She took the mop and bucket and started working. As she mopped her way past the cabinet, she eyed the labels on the drawers. *Powdered sleet. Blizzard balls.* Sarah slipped some in her pocket. Maybe I can use these, she thought.

Suddenly she heard snickering in the doorway.

Jack was standing there. "Well," he said, "if you can't find Old Man Winter, at least you're making yourself useful."

CHAPTER SIX

"Very funny," said Sarah. She put the mop back into the bucket. "I was just pretending in case Kudgel's assistant came back."

"Numlock saw you?"

She grinned. "Is that his name? Don't worry. I let him do most of the talking. But did you have any luck?"

Jack shook his head. "There's no trace. I wish I could think of somewhere special to look. But it's not like Weathermore Castle has a dungeon or anything."

"Are there any maps or drawings of the castle?" asked Sarah. "Maybe they would help."

Jack thought about it. "We could check in the library. There's probably some stuff in there—if we can ever find it buried under all the papers."

The library was in one of the front towers. A round table sat in the middle, surrounded by a few chairs.

The walls were lined with shelves, and though most were filled with books, there were some noticeable gaps. The volumes that belonged there lay scattered across the floor and heaped in piles on the table.

"Kudgel's been in here," said Jack. "Looking for the *Book of Storms*, I expect."

"We'd better work quickly, then," said Sarah. "He might come back at any time. You start with the table. I'll take the shelves."

As she walked over to the bookcase nearest the window, she noticed the white lacy patterns that covered the glass.

"I've never seen frost like that," she said. "It's beautiful."

Jack smiled. "Thank you. I've been practicing."

They worked in silence for a while. Sarah was hoping to see something like *Advanced Castle Design* or *Weathermore Castle: The Complete Plans*. Unfortunately, no such book caught her eye.

She had worked her way through two shelves when she came to a tall black book with nothing written on the spine. She tried to pull it out, but the book wouldn't move.

"Jack, come help me with this."

"Coming."

The two of them grabbed the book together and pulled. The book, however, didn't slide off the shelf. Instead, it tipped down, like a lever.

Suddenly they heard stones grating on one another as a section of curved wall slid away, revealing a hidden alcove.

Jack gasped in surprise. "I didn't know that was there. And I've been here a hundred times."

They rushed over. The alcove was barely big enough to hold them both. In the middle a book lay open on a tall stand. The book was bound in blue leather, and its pages were faintly cool to the touch.

"It's the *Book of Storms*," Jack whispered.

Sarah glanced down at the open page. It appeared to contain recipes, but instead of flour or eggs or butter, the ingredients included *snow salt*, *minced icicles*, and *dehydrated sleet*.

"I can't believe we found it," Sarah said.

Then she frowned. "Old Man Winter was saying that Kudgel would never truly succeed without the *Book of Storms*."

"Well, we'd better unfind it," said Jack, "before Kudgel finds out."

"I thought I heard someone in here."

Jack and Sarah both jumped at the sudden voice. They turned to see Kudgel and Numlock standing in the doorway.

"What do you think you're doing?" Kudgel asked. He did not look pleased.

"Um, just cleaning up, Master Kudgel," Jack explained quickly. He stepped in front of the pedestal, hoping to block it from Kudgel's view.

"I don't remember asking you to do that. And who's this?" He pointed to Sarah.

"The new servant girl," said Numlock. But he was frowning as well.

"Well, servant girls don't belong in the library. "And . . . What's that?"

Jack just shrugged, but Kudgel rushed forward, pushing Jack and Sarah aside.

"The *Book of Storms!*" he murmured, eagerly flipping through the cold pages. He closed the book and hugged it to his chest. "Come, Numlock!"

"What about *them?*"

"They're not important." He wagged a finger at Sarah. "You, girl, just keep your mind on your work. And as for you—" He scowled at Jack. "If you're lucky, I'll keep you on as a stable boy. Understand?"

"Yes, sir," Jack mumbled, looking at the floor.

"Let's go, Numlock," said Kudgel. He clutched the book tightly. "With this book I can create such destruction in the Kettles and The Outland that everyone will fear the name of the Winter King."

He rushed out, with Numlock scurrying along at his heels.

Sarah and Jack stared at each other in shock.

"I'm sure things could be worse," said Jack, after a long minute had passed.

Sarah wished it were true, but she couldn't see how. Maybe she had been wrong to come. Maybe the time hadn't been right for a visit to the Kettles. She had only wanted to help Old Man Winter, and all she had done was give Kudgel the one thing he needed to make his evil plan complete.

CHAPTER SEVEN

"Are you sure about this?" asked Jack.

He and Sarah were standing at the bottom of a flight of stairs that led down from the castle courtyard.

"No, I'm not sure," she admitted, looking through an iron gate into the moat. "But we have to get that book back somehow. We need a distraction—and a polar bear is the biggest distraction I can think of. If we can lure it up the stairs into the courtyard, Kudgel and Numlock will have to deal with it. While they do that, we can steal the book and hide it again."

"All right," said Jack. "We'll try it." He opened the gate and poked his head into the moat. Then he whistled.

A few moments later the polar bear lumbered into view.

"Over here!" Jack shouted, propping the gate

open. He held up a half-frozen fish and waved it around.

The bear roared at them.

"I believe we have its attention," said Jack. He dropped the fish on the bottom step.

They ran up the stairs and crossed the main courtyard. On the far side they ducked behind an archway—and waited. It wasn't long before the polar bear appeared.

"Go on!" said Sarah whispered. "Growl. Roar. Make some noise."

But the bear had stopped. It sniffed at the stones and then began padding out toward them.

"Uh-oh," said Jack.

"But why would the bear come to us?" Sarah wondered. She stared at Jack. "It must have picked up your scent."

"I don't have a scent," he protested.

Sarah took a deep breath. "Oh, really? Then what's that smell?"

Jack took a sniff. Then his face turned white as he reached into his pocket. "I forgot about the other fish."

He quickly threw the fish into the courtyard. The bear stopped, sniffed, and then ambled toward it.

Sarah and Jack held their breaths.

The bear swallowed the fish whole—and let out a growl. Then it began loping toward them.

"Run!" cried Jack.

The stairs behind them led down in a long spiral. The children scrambled along it, steadying

themselves on the rough stone walls.

After a minute or so they stopped to listen. They heard nothing.

"Where does this lead?" Sarah asked.

Jack tried to think. "The only thing I remember down here is the furnace for the Weather Mill."

Sarah wiped her forehead. "No wonder it's getting warmer."

A low growl caught their attention.

"The bear's still coming," said Jack. "Let's go!"

At the bottom of the stairs there was a small hallway. A thick wooden door stood directly before them. It had a barred opening near the top.

"Now what?" asked Sarah.

"Who's there?" a voice cried out weakly from behind the door.

The door was locked, but Sarah and Jack stood on tiptoes to peer through the opening.

"Oh!" they cried together.

At the back of the room was the furnace, glowing dully. And sitting on the floor before it in a steaming puddle of water was Old Man Winter.

"Master!" Jack cried.

"Are you okay?" asked Sarah.

Old Man Winter pointed toward the wall. "The keys!" he said faintly.

Jack looked around and saw an iron key hanging from a peg. He took it down and unlocked the door.

The heat from the furnace nearly smothered them as they entered the room and hurried to Old Man Winter's side.

"Can you walk?" asked Sarah.

Old Man Winter struggled to his feet. "I'll need some help," he admitted. "The heat robs me of my

strength, as Kudgel well knows. He was more clever than I gave him credit for."

Jack stepped forward. He pressed his hand gently against his master's forehead, leaving behind a compress made of frost.

"That's better," said Old Man Winter. "Thank you, Jack."

"We need to go now," said Sarah. "I'm hoping there's another way out, because the way we came in is blocked."

"Blocked by what?" asked Old Man Winter.

There was a growl behind them as the bear lumbered down the last of the stairs.

Sarah gasped. The door! They had forgotten to shut it.

The bear shuffled forward, heading straight for Old Man Winter. Jack tried to pull his master to the side, but he was in no condition to run.

Sarah screamed.

The bear ignored her. It moved closer and closer to Old Man Winter. Their noses almost touched.

And then the bear licked his face.

"Yes, yes," Old Man Winter said gently. "I'm glad to see you, too."

CHAPTER EIGHT

"The bear likes you!" said Sarah in surprise.

"Of course," said Old Man Winter. "We've been friends for a long time."

"But the bear guards the castle," Jack objected. "You never told me it was friendly."

"Shouldn't a guard bear be fierce and scary?" asked Sarah.

Old Man Winter snorted. "Doesn't it look fierce and scary?"

Sarah had to admit this was true.

"Well, that's usually enough." He fixed his gaze on her. "Have we met?" he asked.

Sarah felt her face flush. "Um, yes. It was earlier today. At The Magic Door."

"Ah, now I remember." Old Man Winter nodded. "You're a friend of Sam's from The Outland. But Sarah, how did you get here?"

Sarah felt her blush grow hotter. "I, well, I hitched a ride in the back of your wagon."

"In my wagon?" Old Man Winter looked positively astonished. Then he let out a great laugh.

"My first stowaway," he cried, shaking his head. "But why?"

"I wanted to see the Kettles again."

"Is that all? Hasn't Sam told you that it's not a trip to take lightly?"

Sarah sighed. "Yes, I know, and maybe he was right. But I couldn't help myself. And I wanted to help, but all I did was make things worse."

"Worse?" Old Man Winter frowned. "You helped Jack find me, didn't you? What have you made worse?"

"It wasn't all Sarah's fault," said Jack. "We were in the library, and we found the *Book of Storms*."

Sarah sighed. "And then Kudgel came in." They explained what had happened, and why they had set the polar bear free.

Old Man Winter frowned. "If I know Kudgel, he's planning his next storm right now. We have to stop him!" He took a step forward but tottered unsteadily. "I'm still too weak. It's the heat from that blasted furnace."

Jack suddenly smiled. "That's right! But what if we made it even hotter?"

Both Sarah and Old Man Winter stared at him.

"I'm not crazy," Jack insisted. "Think about it . . . the furnace powers the Weather Mill. What if we built the fire up until it overheated? Wouldn't that shut the Mill down?"

Old Man Winter nodded. "It would indeed. But we would have to overheat it quickly. Coal wouldn't do that."

"Wait," said Sarah, digging in her pockets. "I collected these while I was cleaning. I was going to ask you about them."

Old Man Winter took a quick look. "Hmmm, not the *ice fluff*. Ah, *storm yeast* and *freeze-dried lightning*! These might just work."

The furnace roared as the ingredients were thrown in, sending a great pulse of heat up the air shafts toward the Weather Mill itself.

Kudgel, who at that moment was standing in front of the main controls, did not notice the change. He was too busy studying one of the pages in the *Book of Storms*.

"The moment has come," he said. "With this book as a guide, I will make the greatest storm there has ever been. Mark my words, Numlock, people will tremble before the power of the Winter King."

He nodded to his assistant, who pulled the biggest lever on the Weather Mill. The great machine sprang into life, the gears grinding and pistons hissing.

"Soon the world will see my true power," said Kudgel. "I will be famous, respected . . . and feared."

Numlock was staring at one of the dials. "Master?"

Kudgel glared at him. "Quiet! This is a turning point in history! You don't interrupt turning points."

"I'm sorry, Master, truly sorry. But the temperature is rising much too fast."

"Well, don't just stand there jabbering. Do something about it!"

Numlock tried. He pulled levers and pressed buttons. He even peered into the chutes. "I can't make it stop," he protested. "It's . . . it's . . . like the furnace is putting out too much heat. If this keeps up, the Weather Mill will explode."

Kudgel stormed over to check for himself. "That's not possible." He frowned. "He's loose. The old man is loose. I don't know how, but he must be."

"Old Man Winter?" Numlock shivered. "If he catches us, he'll turn us into overgrown icicles for sure. What can we do? Should I go find some more barrels of water?"

Kudgel shook his head. "I doubt he'll fall for that trick again."

"Then what?"

Kudgel snapped the *Book of Storms* shut and tucked it under his arm. "We'll just have to think of something."

Kudgel strode toward the stairway in the corner of the Storm Chamber. Whimpering with fear, Numlock hurried after him.

CHAPTER NINE

Sarah and Jack helped Old Man Winter up the steps into the courtyard.

"Look!" cried Jack. Black smoke was spilling out of an upper window.

Old Man Winter took a deep breath. "Now that we're in the open air, I can feel my strength returning. But we must hurry. Stopping Kudgel is important, but I don't want the Weather Mill destroyed."

When they reached the Weather Mill, the room was deserted and the machine was rattling noisily.

Old Man Winter marched to a bank of levers and quickly disengaged the main shaft from the steaming furnace below.

The rattling faded to a slight rumble as the mill shut down.

Jack frowned. "Where's Kudgel? He must have bolted."

"We cannot permit him to escape with the *Book of Storms*," said Old Man Winter. "Even without the Weather Mill, he could still cause much mischief with the book alone."

Suddenly they heard a creaking noise coming from the ceiling.

"The Overlook!" cried Old Man Winter. "Someone's preparing for a launch." He rushed toward the stairs.

Sarah and Jack ran after him.

"What's the Overlook?" she asked.

"It's outside the High Tower," Jack explained. "The catapult is there. Old Man Winter uses it to launch ice seedlings into the clouds."

When they reached the door to the Overlook, it was locked. They could hear muffled voices coming from the other side.

"Open this door!" Old Man Winter commanded.

Nobody answered his call.

"Let me try," said Jack.

He brushed his fingers lightly over the keyhole, filling it with frost. Then he knelt down and blew on it softly. As Sarah and Old Man Winter watched, the metal plate around the keyhole bulged outward.

"Step back," cautioned Jack.

A moment later the entire lock burst into splinters.

Old Man Winter grunted. "That's not something I taught you."

Jack grinned. Then he gave the door a push.

Sarah was startled by the sudden view. The Overlook was a wide balcony that loomed high above the countryside. At the far end was a giant catapult. And sitting in the cup that normally held sacks of ice seedlings were Kudgel and Numlock.

"Get down from there!" ordered Old Man Winter.

"I no longer obey your orders!" Kudgel snarled. He took hold of a long metal lever.

Old Man Winter folded his arms. "I won't let you get away with this."

Kudgel laughed. "How will you stop me, old man?"

While he had been speaking, Sarah had moved slowly around behind him. When she reached the ledge of the balcony, she found it covered in wet snow.

Old Man Winter looked sadly at Kudgel. "This is madness," he warned.

"We shall see," Kudgel spat. "While I have the book, I am still a force to be reckoned with!"

He held the *Book of Storms* high in the air, taunting Old Man Winter. Suddenly a snowball smashed against his hand, knocking the book loose. It skittered safely across the floor and came to rest in front of Old Man Winter.

Kudgel scowled at Sarah, who was readying another snowball just in case. "You have not seen the last of me," he snarled.

Then he pulled the lever.

With a loud *swoosh* the catapult whipped forward, sending Kudgel and Numlock headlong into the sky. Numlock's last scream hung in the air as they sailed toward the horizon.

Sarah rushed to the wall. "Where will they end up?" she gasped.

"Judging by the angle, I would guess Tarpaulin Bay," said Old Man Winter. He picked up the *Book of Storms*. "It will be a very wet landing."

"That was a nice shot, Sarah," Jack said admiringly.

"Thanks. Your trick with the lock was pretty good, too. How did you do that?"

"He can explain it to you on the way to Moon Haven," said Old Man Winter. The port town was about an hour's ride away. "Take the wagon, Jack, and see that she gets safely to her friend Sam's toy shop. It connects with his other shop in The Outland."

Jack was disappointed that Sarah was leaving so soon. "You never got to meet my winter gullhare," he said sadly. "Or go flying with me."

"You can fly?"

He nodded. "On the back of the gullhare. It's how I spread the frost. You'll come back to try it sometime, won't you?"

Sarah sighed. "I certainly hope so," she said.

CHAPTER TEN

As Sarah closed the magic door in Sam's toy shop, she saw Sam, Michael, and Joey sitting at the long bench. They were hunched over a drawing Michael had made of a weather machine.

"I'd pour the ingredients in one end," Michael was explaining, "and shoot them out the other like confetti."

Sarah stole up behind them. "That's very interesting," she said quietly.

"Sarah!" cried Sam, glancing from her to the magic door. "I thought you went to the library."

"I was planning to," Sarah said. "Honest."

"What have I told you about visiting the Kettles?"

"I can explain all that," Sarah said quickly. "Really I can."

Sam crossed his arms. "I'll give you that chance," he said sternly.

"Well, at least there was a happy ending," said Sarah. "That should count for something."

"A happy ending to what?" asked Joey.

Sarah told them.

"I can't believe it!" Michael exclaimed. "You got to help Old Man Winter while I just shoveled my driveway. I wish I could have gone too."

"There's always next time," said Sarah, glancing hopefully at Sam. "Anyway, at least I brought back something for our weather project."

She took three crystals out of her pocket and placed them on the table. "This is *freeze-dried lightning*," she explained.

"Really?" said Michael. "It looks like glittery rock candy. Do you know how to make it work?"

Sarah nodded. "Old Man Winter showed me. The crystals will work only one time, but we'll beat Cordelia this year for sure."

"Just make sure you don't mention where they're from," Sam reminded her.

"Don't worry. Oh, I almost forgot. I brought you something too, Joey." Sarah took what looked like a large clear stone out of her pocket and handed it to him.

"What is it?" asked Joey. It felt cold to the touch.

"Frost-forged ice. So cold, it won't melt even on the hottest day. Old Man Winter uses it to make his ice dome."

Michael frowned. "Ice dome? I can see you haven't told us *everything* yet."

"Well . . ." Sarah hesitated. "We've still got a lot of work to do on our project."

"It can wait," said Michael. "Have a seat."

Sarah sat down. Michael and Joey leaned toward her. Even Sam shifted a little closer.

"All right," said Sarah, and she started from the beginning.